YS PRICE

NORMAN PRICE

BELLA LASAGNE

JAMES

SARAH

MEET ALL THESE FRIENDS IN BUZZ BOOKS:

Thomas the Tank Engine
Fireman Sam
Joshua Jones
Flintstones
Bugs Bunny
Looney Tunes
Tiny Toon Adventures

First published in Great Britain 1990 by Buzz Books,
an imprint of Reed Consumer Books Limited
Michelin House, 81 Fulham Road, London SW3 6RB
and Auckland, Melbourne, Singapore and Toronto

Reprinted 1991, 1992

Fireman Sam copyright © Prism Art & Design Ltd
Text copyright © 1990 Reed International Books Ltd
Illustrations copyright © 1990 Reed International Books Ltd
Story by Caroline Hill-Trevor
Illustrations by CLIC!
Based on the animation series produced by Bumper Films for
S4C/Channel 4 Wales and Prism Art & Design Ltd
Original idea by Dave Gingell and Dave Jones,
assisted by Mike Young. Characters created by Rob Lee.
All rights reserved.

ISBN 1 85591 009 8

A CIP catalogue record for this book is available at the British Library.

Printed and bound in the UK by BPCC Hazell Books Ltd

NORMAN'S SPOOKY NIGHT

Story by Caroline Hill-Trevor
Illustrations by CLIC!

It was Hallowe'en and Bella had promised
Sarah and James that they could have a
party in her café. Everyone in Pontypandy
was invited and there was a prize for the
best fancy dress.

"Hurry up, Sarah," said James after
lunch. "We've got a lot to do before the
guests arrive: decorate the café, lay out the
food and put on our costumes. I hope
Norman's thought of some good tricks."

As the twins were chatting to Bella,
Fireman Sam arrived.

"Would you like some help, you two?"
he asked. "It's my day off and I've got lots
of good ideas for a Hallowe'en party."

"Thanks, Uncle Sam," said Sarah.
"Norman said he'd help, but we can't find
him anywhere. Do you know any good
games?"

8

"Right," said Fireman Sam, taking charge.
"James, you run and buy a pumpkin from
Mrs Price's shop – the biggest you can find
– and Sarah, ask Bella if we can borrow her
big washing-up bowl for apple bobbing."

10

"Great," said James. "I'm brilliant at making pumpkin lanterns, and Sarah's an expert at apple bobbing. Do you know any really scary tricks, Uncle Sam?"

"Oh yes, lots!" Fireman Sam replied.

Sarah and James were so busy planning their party, and chatting to Fireman Sam about Hallowe'en tricks, that neither of them noticed Norman peeking round the door, listening to their conversation.

"Hum," he thought to himself, "that's given me some good ideas. I know what'll really scare them!" And he crept off before anyone saw him.

"This is going to be the best ever pumpkin lantern," boasted James, scooping out an enormous pumpkin.

"What have you put in that water, Sarah?" asked Fireman Sam, pointing at the apples bobbing around in a sea of red water. "It looks just like blood!"

"Don't worry, Uncle Sam, it's only food colouring!" said Sarah, grinning.

Then suddenly all the lights went out. "Now what's going on?" said Fireman Sam. "Don't move, I'll see what's happened."

"This is creepy," said James.

14

After a moment the lights came on again.

"The master switch was turned off," said
Fireman Sam, looking puzzled. "Very
strange." Then the curtains started flapping.
"It's a wild night out there, isn't it. Hey,
wait a minute! All the windows are open.

16

You shouldn't open the windows like that,
you two, it's a waste of heating.''

"But we didn't, Uncle Sam,'' squeaked
Sarah. "It must be a ghost! I'm scared.''

"Don't be silly, Sarah, there are no such things as ghosts," said James.

"Of course there aren't," agreed Fireman Sam. As he spoke Bella came running in.

"Mamma mia! Save me! There's a ghost upstairs," she cried. "I've seen him with my own eyes and poor Rosa, she's run away."

"This is *really* spooky," shivered James.

"I don't believe in ghosts," said
Fireman Sam. "Where's Norman? Did you
say you couldn't find him?"

Suddenly Norman came rushing in, white
as a sheet.

"Hello, Norman. What happened to
you?" asked James.

"There's a ghost in the café," he said.

"Yes, Norman, a lot of strange things
have been happening around here, haven't
they?" agreed Fireman Sam.

"But this one is real," said Norman
sheepishly. "The pumpkin is moving, and it
has green eyes, honest it has," he gasped.

"That's impossible," said James. "I left the pumpkin propped up on the table." As they were talking, Trevor Evans arrived, wearing a white sheet and a green mask.

"Well, here's your ghost, Norman," said Fireman Sam. "Well done, Trevor, that's a

very good fancy dress costume – you
should win a prize.''

"No, Trevor's not the ghost,'' insisted
Norman. "I promise you, that pumpkin has
a life of its own. Go and see for yourselves if
you don't believe me.''

"Well, we'd better have a look then," said
Fireman Sam suspiciously. And sure
enough, when they went through into the
café, the pumpkin lantern which James had
made was moving on its own. In the dim
light, they could see two green eyes looking
out at them.

24

"That's a brilliant trick," said James. "Tell
me how you do it, please, Norman." But
Norman was shaking with fear.

"I promise this is no trick," he groaned.
"The lights, the windows, the ghost upstairs
– they were all me – but there's a real ghost
in that pumpkin, no kidding."

"Rosa," called Bella. "My poor Rosa, she's so frightened of ghosts, we must find her."

"Hold on a moment, Bella," said Fireman Sam. "I think I know where we can find Rosa." He lifted off the top of the pumpkin, and out jumped Rosa!

"I think Rosa should win the prize for the most frightening Hallowe'en costume!" said Fireman Sam, and the others agreed. When all the guests had arrived they turned the lights out and lit the pumpkin lantern. Everyone took a turn at apple bobbing, and James practised his Hallowe'en tricks on everyone except Norman – he'd had enough frights for one day!

FIREMAN SAM

STATION OFFICER
STEELE

TREVOR EVANS

ELVIS
CRIDLINGTON